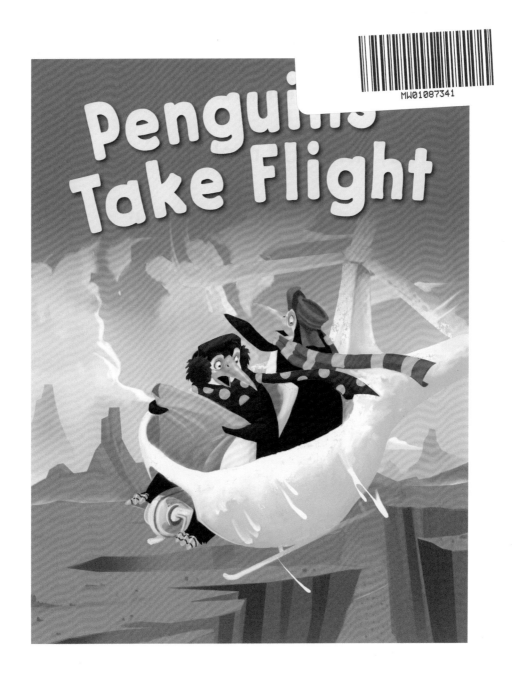

Penguins Take Flight

By Joe Rhatigan

Illustrated by Daniel Whisker

"I need a vacation," Linda said.

"Me too," Marcus replied.

They flapped their wings but
got nowhere.
Oh well, at least they tried.

Linda said, "I have an idea!
Let's build a flyer made of ice.
We'll fly to the Statue of Liberty."

Marcus agreed the trip would be nice.

Linda drew up her plans.
She shaped the ice all around.

Marcus made blades for the tail.

Then, they lifted off the ground.

Marcus said he knew the way.

But his sense of direction was poor.

They ended up over the Grand Canyon.

And then on the California shore.

They landed on the Gateway Arch.
They got out to stretch and rest.

Linda said, "Isn't this place great?
Here, penguins could make nests!"

They traveled onward across the country.

They saw some green up ahead.

"It's the Statue of Liberty," said Linda.

But Marcus looked up in dread.

"The flyer is melting!" said Marcus.
"Oh no, there goes a blade!"

Who knew it would be so hot?
It was 97 degrees in the shade!

A flock of pigeons saved the day.

They plucked them out of the sky.

They dropped them on the statue's torch.

Then they waved a cheerful goodbye.

Linda said, "We did it! We made it!
There is the statue's crown!"

Marcus said, "Now it's time to go home.
But how will we get down?"

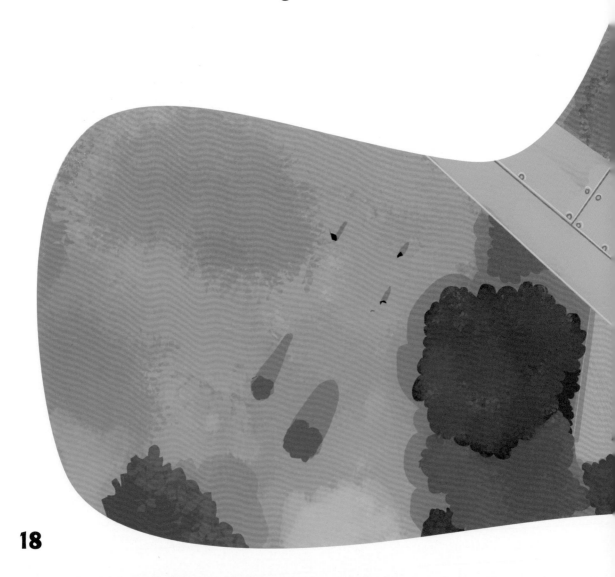

Consultant

Theresa Blue
Resource Specialist
Sierra Sands Unified School District, California

Publishing Credits

Rachelle Cracchiolo, M.S.Ed., *Publisher*
Emily R. Smith, M.A.Ed., *VP of Content Development*
Véronique Bos, *Creative Director*

Image Credits:
Illustrated by Daniel Whisker

Library of Congress Cataloging-in-Publication Data

Names: Rhatigan, Joe, author. | Whisker, Dan, illustrator.
Title: Penguins take flight / by Joe Rhatigan ; illustrated by Daniel Whisker.
Description: Huntington Beach, CA : Teacher Created Materials, [2022] | Includes book club questions. | Audience: Grades K-1.
Identifiers: LCCN 2020006495 (print) | LCCN 2020006496 (ebook) | ISBN 9781087601298 (paperback) | ISBN 9781087619330 (ebook)
Subjects: LCSH: Readers (Primary) | Penguins--Juvenile fiction.
Classification: LCC PE1119 .R4637 2020 (print) | LCC PE1119 (ebook) | DDC 428.6/2--dc23
LC record available at https://lccn.loc.gov/2020006495
LC ebook record available at https://lccn.loc.gov/2020006496

TCM | Teacher Created Materials

5482 Argosy Avenue
Huntington Beach, CA 92649
www.tcmpub.com
ISBN 978-1-0876-0129-8
© 2022 Teacher Created Materials, Inc.